Groundwood Books / House of Anansi Press
groundwoodbooks.com

We gratefully acknowledge for their financial support of our publishing
program the Canada Council for the Arts, the Ontario Arts Council and the
Government of Canada.

ONTARIO ARTS COUNCIL
CONSEIL DES ARTS DE L'ONTARIO
an Ontario government agency
un organisme du gouvernement de l'Ontario

With the participation of the Government of Canada
Avec la participation du gouvernement du Canada | Canadä

Nahid Kazemi thanks the Conseil des arts et des lettres du Québec for its
financial support.

Library and Archives Canada Cataloguing in Publication
Title: The old woman / Joanne Schwartz ; pictures by Nahid Kazemi.
Names: Schwartz, Joanne (Joanne F.), author. | Kazemi, Nahid, illustrator.
Identifiers: Canadiana (print) 20190228075 | Canadiana (ebook) 20190228083 |
ISBN 9781773062112 (hardcover) | ISBN 9781773062129 (EPUB) |
ISBN 9781773064260 (Kindle)
Classification: LCC PS8637.C592 O43 2029 | DDC jC813/.6—dc23

The illustrations were created with chalk pastels, color pencils and some
mixed media.
Design by Michael Solomon
Printed and bound in China

To Coal and Sydney,
two good dogs, and to
my mother, with love.
— JS

To my mother,
who has been
a strong woman.
— NK

THE OLD WOMAN

JOANNE SCHWARTZ

PICTURES BY

NAHID KAZEMI

GROUNDWOOD BOOKS
HOUSE OF ANANSI PRESS
TORONTO   BERKELEY

THERE was an old house that didn't have much in it.

An old woman lived there with a scruffy
old dog who was her best friend.

Most mornings the dog
went outside and chased
squirrels around the
old house until he tired
himself out.

Then he curled up on the worn-out rug
and dozed, one eye opening now and again.

One day the old woman and the dog went for a walk into
the hills. It was fall, and the old woman wanted to hear the
crunch of dry leaves under her feet and the wind whispering
through the trees.

It was some time since the old woman and the dog had walked this way, but it was just as she remembered it — the rocks, the trees, and the boulder they were heading toward that made a perfect place to sit down.

The old woman stopped to watch a crow fly past. The dog looked up, too. What would it feel like to fly? she thought. She imagined wings spread, gliding on wind currents. She teetered a bit just thinking about it. To have a bird's-eye view, now that would be something.

On she went, throwing sticks for the dog here
and there. He ran after them and brought them
back, dropping them at her feet.

The old woman spotted a long thick one that would
make a good walking stick. She tried it out — thump,
step, thump, step. That works well, she thought.

After a while she came upon the boulder with its perfect seat and sat down to rest. The dog lay down at her feet, panting from running after sticks. He needed a rest, too.

The wind came up, whirling the leaves in the air. It was getting late. The old woman remembered when she used to play outside for hours, never wanting to go in. Couldn't the day last forever?

The harvest moon rose slowly
and suddenly it was there,
taking her breath away. What
was that word? *Magnificent* — it
was magnificent. And it was so
orange, or sort of a rusty color.

She thought about how to
describe it — huge, looming,
warm, gentle, enormous,
dreamy, peaceful, autumnal —
magnificent.

When they got back to the house, the old woman sat in her chair and put her feet up. She noticed a hole in the curtains. Tomorrow I'll mend them, she thought. She was tired. She closed her eyes and drifted off to sleep. The dog curled up, and soon began to snore.

The old woman woke
up early the next morning.
She felt stiff and achy from
her long walk. She put the
kettle on.

The sky was still dark,
and she could hear birds
chirping outside her
window.

Pulling on a heavy
sweater, she went
outside to sit and
watch the sun rise.
The dog came, too,
and sat by her side.

There was a chill
in the air. Soon it
would be cold.

It always comes
like this, thought
the old woman, and
yet no one day is the
same as another.

The sky was lighter now, the darkness fading. The air feels quiet, if you could say that, she thought, and where it touches my face, it feels like the softest hand in the world.

The day stretched out before her. In her mind's eye the old woman went up the hill again. She didn't seem to feel the time passing, and anyway, she thought, I am not in a hurry.

She smiled at the dog and reached down to pat him.
"It's a new day — what do you think? Shall we
spend it together? I think so, too, my good old friend."

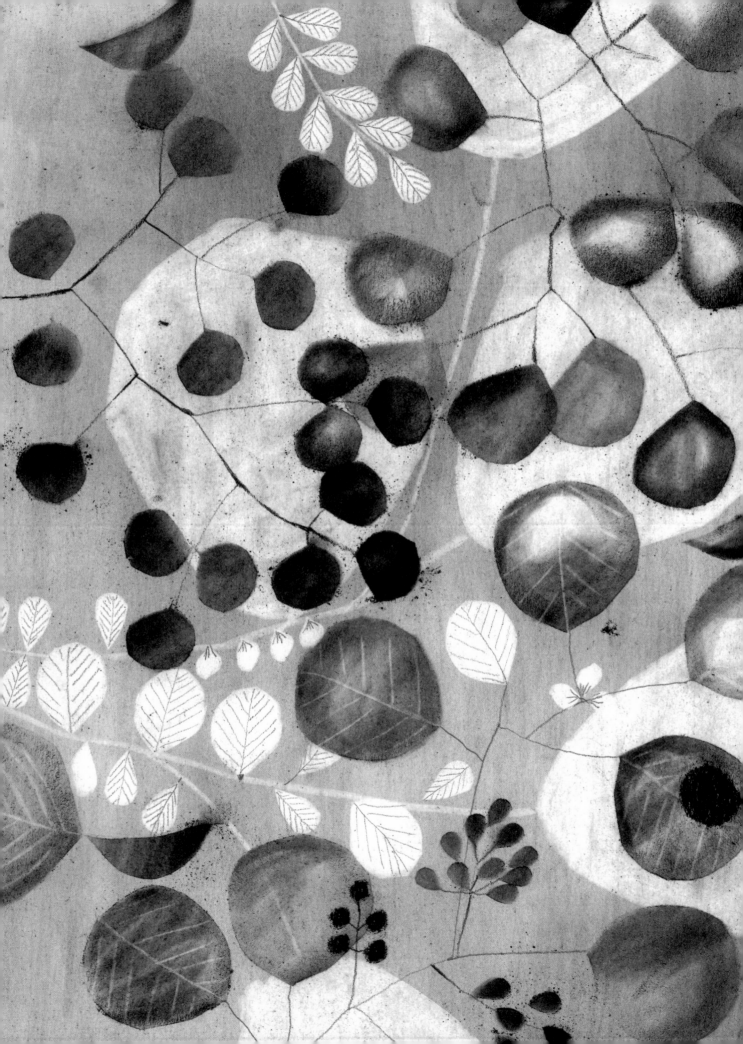